THE

QWIKPICK

PAPERS

POOP FOUNTAIN!

Other books by Tom Angleberger

In the Origami Yoda series
The Strange Case of Origami Yoda
Darth Paper Strikes Back
The Secret of the Fortune Wookiee
Art2-D2's Guide to Folding and Doodling
The Surprise Attack of Jabba the Puppett
Princess Labelmaker to the Rescue!

Fake Mustache: Or, How Jodie O'Rodeo and Her Wonder Horse (and Some Nerdy Kid) Saved the U.S. Presidential Election from a Mad Genius Criminal Mastermind

Horton Halfpott: Or, The Fiendish Mystery of Smugwick Manor; Or, The Loosening of M'Lady Luggertuck's Corset

Amulet Books
New York

THE

QWIKPICK

PAPERS

POOP FOUNTAIN!

Found by
TOM ANGLEBERGER

The illustrations in this book are by Jen Wang.
The photographs are by Tom Angleberger.

Library of Congress Cataloging-in-Publication Data

Angleberger, Tom.
[Qwikpick Adventure Society]
Poop fountain! / by Tom Angleberger ; illustrated by Jen Wang.
pages cm. — (The Qwikpick papers ; [1])
"Previously published by Dial Books for Young Readers in 2007 as
The Qwikpick Adventure Society by Sam Riddleburger"—Copyright page.
Summary: Three friends spend Christmas day breaking into the town of
Crickenburg's antiquated sewage treatment plant in order to witness with their own eyes
the soon-to-be-replaced "poop fountain."
ISBN 978-1-4197-0425-3 (hardback)
[1. Sewage disposal plants—Fiction. 2. Friendship—Fiction. 3. Humorous stories.]
I. Wang, Jen, 1984– illustrator. II. Title.
PZ7.A585Po 2014
[Fic]—dc23
2013045212

Printed and bound in U.S.A.
10 9 8 7 6 5 4 3 2 1

Previously published by Dial Books for Young Readers in 2007
as *The Qwikpick Adventure Society* by Sam Riddleburger.

Amulet Books are available at special discounts when purchased in quantity for premiums and promotions as well as fundraising or educational use. Special editions can also be created to specification. For details, contact specialsales@abramsbooks.com or the address below.

115 West 18th Street
New York, NY 10011
www.abramsbooks.com

This book is dedicated to my favorite writers, including Daniel Pinkwater, Lloyd Alexander, Helen Cresswell, Mervyn Peake, Lynda Barry, Charles Dickens, and, especially, Cece Bell.

An important note to the reader
from Tom Angleberger

Some of you may know that before I wrote the Origami Yoda books I used to be a newspaper reporter. For years I covered everything that happened in this town down in the mountains of Virginia called Crickenburg. And one of the hundreds of stories I wrote was about a big change at the sewage plant. That was around the year 2000, and back then Crickenburg was growing like crazy, and that meant there were a lot more people flushing toilets. So they made the sewage plant bigger.

I had to go down to the sewage plant to interview the plant manager—and, MAN, did it stink! I stayed as far away from the big pools of brown goop as I could! I got the facts and got out of there! Then I wrote them up, and the paper printed them. I thought that was the end of the story.

But just recently I found out that there was a lot more that happened after that. It was a lot crazier, messier, stinkier—and, yes, POOPIER—than I ever knew! A few months ago, this guy called me and told me he had found a big stack of really weird papers in the storage room of the old Qwikpick gas station on Franklin Street. One of the things in the big stack was my story about the sewage plant.

I said I'd like to take a look, and, yes, there was my story, although the newspaper had turned yellow over the years.

It was the rest of the papers that were really interesting, though. They told an absolutely crazy story about these kids trying to go on an adventure. I'll let you read all about it yourself. After all, that's the whole point to reprinting their "official report" in this book. (I haven't been able to find the kids, but I bet they'd be really pleased to know their report got printed up!)

But before you read it, let me tell you what it was like back in 2000 . . .

Kids weren't running around with camera phones. A camera and a phone were two separate things, and most kids didn't have either. Most of their parents didn't have cellphones yet, or, if they did, they spent most of their time complaining that they didn't work very well.

People were just getting used to digital cameras, but they were big and chunky and sometimes the photos were pretty cruddy—plus they were expensive.

Most families had a computer by then, but there wasn't as much to do with it: no YouTube or Twitter, and I think Facebook was maybe just getting started. And the Internet was really slow, so you couldn't watch streaming TV and there was no easy way to download music, either. (I'm having trouble remembering what we DID use computers for back then, actually . . .)

All of this meant that if you lived in a pretty boring town, you couldn't just go online and find something cool to do. You had to try to find something cool in the real world. And that's what these kids had been trying to do.

Did they succeed?

Well, you should find out for yourself.

So I'll stop now and let you start digging into that big crazy stack of papers the dude found at the Qwikpick . . . also known as *The Qwikpick Papers.*

Tom Angleberger

THE

QWIKPICK

PAPERS

The offical report of The Qwikpick Adventure
Society's trip to see the Fountain of Poop

The Qwikpick

SECTION I
The Introduction

This is the report of the first-ever trip of The Qwikpick Adventure Society. It has been written by Lyle Hertzog (me) with the help of co-members Marilla Anderson, who took the pictures, and Dave Raskin, who drew the maps and stuff.

Let me just say that Dave came up with the name for our group and Marilla and I voted for it too, because we thought it was funny.

See, we sometimes hang out at a place called the Qwikpick---a big gas station and convenience store, which is where my mom and dad work. There's a break room with two old sofas, a microwave, and a TV that you have to turn on and off with a screwdriver. It only gets channel seven.

The Qwikpick is down on South Franklin Street right in front of Crab Creek Estates Trailer Park, where I've

lived for a long time and Marilla
just moved to about a year ago.

So that's why we called ourselves
The Qwikpick Adventure Society.
Society is just a fancy word for club,
which is stretching it a bit since
there's only three of us.

But the word adventure is
stretching it a lot.

We didn't stop a smuggling ring
or get mixed up with the mob or stop
an ancient evil from rising up
and spreading black terror across
Crickenburg.

You should not be expecting some
kind of crazy wild adventure. If
that's what you want, then you need to
read The Hoboken Chicken Emergency,
by D. Manus Pinkwater, which is the
greatest book ever written.

But we did see something that not
many other people have gotten to see
and no one will get to see again---
the Amazing Poop Fountain at the
Crickenburg Wastewater Treatment
Plant.

That's why we decided to record our experience for future people to read so they will know what the poop fountain was like and also what it was like to go see it AND SMELL IT!!!

By the way, this report has been typed on a typewriter becau se Lyle Hertzog (me) got a typewriter for Christmas.

my typewriter

UNOFFICIAL personal note

Of course, I didn't tell Dave and Marilla the real story about getting the typewriter.

Obviously I didn't really want a typewriter, I wanted a computer.

Every kid I know has got a computer or at least a video game player. So when I saw this big plastic case next to the Christmas tree, I thought I was finally getting one or the other.

When I opened it up, I saw the keyboard and I was for one second about to flip out. Then I realized that there was no screen, just the keys and a few big knobs and some clunky metal levers.

"It's a typewriter," my dad said. "This man came in the Qwikpick and asked if he could put up a sign on the bulletin board because he had a typewriter to sell and I was like, 'How much do you want? Because my son would love to have a typewriter.'"

It's true that I've been saying that I'd like to be a newspaper reporter someday, but I always figured I'd be writing stories on a computer, not a typewriter. My class took a field trip to a newspaper office one time and I didn't see any typewriters.

The typewriter is heavier than you would believe and it makes a loud buzzing noise when it's plugged in. But I do like the whack-whack-whack when you type, and it has this white ribbon that lets you erase mistakes. That's how come it looks like I'm typing perfectly when I'm not at all. Really, it took me forever just to type that first part.

SECTION II
Founding Members:
Marilla Anderson,
Dave H. Raskin,
Lyle Hertzog (me)

Marilla has asked me to say right away that she isn't the girlfriend of either one of us. Nor will she fall in love with either one of us during the course of the events that are typed up in this document.

The three of us have been friends for a little over a year, but we didn't create The Qwikpick Adventure Society until just a few weeks before Christmas.

One day at school when kids were talking about Christmas stuff, the three of us realized that none of us had anything much to do on Christmas Day.

Another personal note: I have liked Marilla for a long time now and so just because she says she doesn't fall in love with either one of us, do not give up hope! Wheels will be set in motion!

7

Marilla's family is Jehovah's Witnesses. This is a religion that believes in Christ but does not celebrate Christmas. A lot of people complain about them because on some weekends they knock on people's doors and talk about religion. However, Marilla is perfectly nice. She lives in the same trailer park as I do, Crab Creek Estates. She used to live in a town house before her father got a kidney condition and had to quit his job.

So, anyway, she wasn't going to do anything for Christmas except hang around the house watching videos, and she's not allowed to watch anything that's PG-13 or R, and she says that if she has to watch The Lion King with her little sister one more time she'll barf.

Dave's family is Jewish and by the time school lets out for Christmas break he's usually already had Hanukkah and visited his grandparents and everything.

Dave's twin brothers are only one year older than him, but they are twice as big as he is and are always beating him up and bossing him around.

On Christmas Day he and his stepfather and his twin brothers were probably going to sit around and watch a football bowl game on TV.

But Dave doesn't really like football or his two brothers, so he wanted to get out of his house too.

And as for me, my parents both have to work at the Qwikpick on Christmas Day. The Qwikpick closes early on Christmas Eve, but then opens up at five in the morning on Christmas Day. And they have a policy that all employees, except the mana ger, have to work because Christmas Day is a day when lots of people travel, and that means that they buy gas and biscuits, and that means my parents can never take that day off.

UNOFFICIAL personal note

My mother is the assistant manager and maybe someday she'll be a full manager and will get Christmas Day off. My father is just a cashier and biscuit-maker. (Around here, any decent convenience store sells biscuits—egg biscuits, ham biscuits, and especially gravy and biscuits—in the morning starting really early.)

He used to have a better job in the warehouse at the FabriTec plant. The plant closed down about seven years ago and was torn down and Kroger built a supermarket where it used to be. My father refuses to shop there even though it's closer than the Food Lion where we do shop.

Anyway, he couldn't find another job, so my mom got him a job at the Qwikpick with her.

fried baloney with cheese!

My parents always volunteer to work a double shift on Christmas because they get extra holiday pay. So we have our Christmas dinner and open our presents on Christmas Eve. It's no big deal to spend Christmas Day alone, because I'm used to spending a lot of time by myself. I figured I'd probably watch some movies.

But when we realized that we all had nothing to do on Christmas, Dave, Marilla, and I started thinking that we could do something a lot more fun.

"On Christmas morning all the parks and basketball courts and playgrounds are totally empty," Dave said. "We could have them all to ourselves without a bunch of jerks around hogging everything."

"It's not just the parks," said Marilla. "Except for the churches, the whole town will be empty. We could probably sneak around behind the shops downtown and find all kinds of cool stuff."

"That sounds awesome," I said, "but not downtown. I've looked around down there before. The only cool thing I've ever seen is that fifty-gallon drum behind the empty old Kroger store that says 'Banana Puree.'"

"Well, we could see what's in it," said Marilla.

"I'd rather not," said Dave. "Some things should remain a mystery."

"Ha, ha," said Marilla. "Anyway, I bet we could do something cool and not get caught. After all, the cops are all going to be watching holiday traffic on the bypass."

"And eating biscuits at the Qwikpick," I added.

"What do you mean about cops?" asked Dave. "I'm not going to do anything that would get me in trouble."

Dave is the number-one rule-follower of all time. In PE when we run laps around the gym, he makes sure that he runs to all four corners. Meanwhile, the rest of us are running in a circle around the middle of the gym, so he always finishes last.

"Well, I don't mean stealing or doing anything bad, obviously," said Marilla, "but, you know, maybe going somewhere we haven't been invited to go. Somewhere that we could never go with our parents. Somewhere that nobody else goes."

"Somewhere over the rainbow?" said Dave.

"I'm serious," she said. "This is our chance to go somewhere great."

"But where?" I asked.

None of us could think of anything perfect, but we agreed that if we couldn't think of anything better we would go see if we could open the banana puree. That didn't seem great but Marilla said it would be better than watching The Lion King for the million th time.

But then we heard about something even better than fifty gallons of old, squished bananas--twenty million gallons of sewage!

the big can of
banana puree

UNOFFICIAL SECTION II and a half

Before we get to the sewage, I'm going to write the story about how Marilla, Dave, and I met.

See, before I started hanging around with them, I really didn't have any good friends.

Now, I'm not writing this down to be a whiner, but only to tell the whole truth and nothing but the truth. Believe me, I'd rather write down that I had lots of friends.

The funny thing is that I can tell you what the problem was, but I couldn't seem to do anything to fix that problem.

Most of the kids at school don't like me because they think I'm stuck-up and that I think I'm smarter than everybody else. I know this because last year Tonya Felman hissed those exact words across the room at me just because I got excited about getting an A on something.

Well, I shouldn't have said anything about my grade, and believe me, I never do anymore, but I think Tonya is wrong.

I'm not stuck-up and I don't think I'm smarter than everybody else. (Well, I am smarter than Tonya, but she doesn't even try.)

It's the same way that I think Kevin Morris is stuck-up about how good he plays basketball. Maybe he's not. Maybe he's just proud to be good at something, like I am. That still doesn't excuse him from slapping the ball out of my hands and yelling "Rejected" and "Not in my house" all the time. I don't yell that when I beat him on a spelling test.

Perhaps the biggest problem with having no friends is that you have no one to save a seat for you in the cafeteria. Because then when you try to find a seat, there's always some pushy girl going "That's saved." They say it with such a nasty tone that you feel like you asked her out on a date and she said she'd rather die.

So go back in time almost a whole year ago. One day I had gotten three "That's saved"s in a row when I saw a seat next to Marilla.

Now, normally I would never have talked to Marilla because I have always liked her and that makes me extra afraid of her. I'm surprised that most guys don't think she's the prettiest girl in our grade, because I do. I guess they like the girls with makeup and hairstyles and clothes that show their belly buttons. Marilla doesn't do any of that.

Even though I've gotten to know her better, I've never really figured out exactly what she is. I mean as far as being black or white or whatever. Both of her parents look white, but she doesn't exactly. I've never had the nerve to ask her about it. In fact, up till then I'd never had the nerve to speak to her at all.

But there was no place else to sit, so I went over there with my tray and I asked her and I didn't get rejected.

Marilla just said, "Sure."

She was sitting on the edge of the nerd table, which is a table you'd think I'd already be sitting at, but I wasn't because of Jeremy Price, a kid who is stuck-up and thinks he's smarter than everybody else. I think he sees me as competition and so he's always giving me a hard time.

But Jeremy was on the other end of the group from Marilla and was busy repeating the plot of <u>Terminator 2</u> for probably the millionth time.

Besides Jeremy, there are a bunch of other guys who are all in the school band, like Mark, Ian, and Isak, who mostly sit around and complain about everybody else in the entire school.

Then there's Elizabeth, also in the band, who Marilla hangs around with all the time. She and Marilla can do cat's cradle faster than anyone.

And, of course, Dave also sits at the nerd table. We were already sort of friends because in PE we spent a lot of time on the bleachers together waiting to get subbed into basketball games.

I could never figure out why he looked a little strange. Then one day I found my dad's old high school yearbook, from like 1978. The boys in it all looked and dressed like Dave. I guess he would have been cool if he had been born forty years earlier.

So when I sat down next to Marilla, I kind of said hey to Dave. But I expected that they'd keep talking to their friends and I would just eat lunch without talking to anybody like usual. But then Marilla started talking to me.

"Hey, do you live in the Crab Creek trailers?" Marilla asked.

"Yeah," I said. I've always been sensitive about living in a trailer because a lot of people are trailer bigots. They think there's something wrong with you if you live in a trailer.

"I'm going to be moving there in a few weeks," she said. "As soon as my parents sell our house."

"Really?" I said in a way that was obviously too happy for what she probably considered bad news.

"Yeah, so I hope it's all right there. Do you like it?"

This was obviously not the time to tell her about the guy with the world's loudest car who goes to work at 4:30 in the morning. Or the family that keeps a dog chained up outside all year round and it barks all the time.

Or the fact that my parents' dream is to get enough money to move out of there.

My mom says that when we pay off the credit cards we may be able to get a double-wide trailer out in the county. That would be awesome. Sometimes on TV people make jokes about double-wides, but those people have obviously never lived in a single-wide.

But if Marilla was moving to the trailer park, I realized, it might suddenly become a great place to live.

So I tried to make it sound pretty good.

"It's pretty good," I said. "There's a lot of streets to ride your bike on and there's some trees and some nice old people who live there. Plus, the Qwikpick is right there and it has an old Ms. Pac-Man machine that you can play for free."

"Really? What's your high score?"

"Um, about 28,000 something," I said.

"Mine's 42,736," she said. "I used to play at the bowling alley when my dad used to bowl."

Then Dave said that he had never played Ms. Pac-Man, but he was pretty sure he could do better than 42,736 because he could score a million points on some PlayStation game. Marilla said, "Yeah, right."

We talked about other stuff too, like the dumb movie Mr. Michaels had made everybody watch in Life Science class and Dave's comic book he was working on (The All-Zombie Marching Band) and Marilla's map of Canada she made for social studies class, which had blinking Christmas tree lights on it in the shape of Quebec.

Everybody else was talking about the Super Bowl coming up that weekend, but we all agreed that it was stupid and football was stupid and the Redskins' mascot was stupid.

Unfortunately, Jeremy heard me saying something and hollered down the table, "Hey, if we wanted any of your crap, I'd beat it out of you."

"Shove it, Jeremy," said Dave, which was the nicest thing anyone had ever said in my honor.

When it was time to go, Marilla said, "Hey, if you want, I'll save this seat for you tomorrow."

That was when, without them even knowing it, Marilla and Dave became my best friends.

Not long after that, Marilla moved into the trailer park and started riding my bus. When she didn't have to babysit her sister, we would sometimes hang around the Qwikpick until supper time. Then Dave started riding the bus home with us sometimes and hanging out too.

Summer, which was usually totally boring for me, was awesome this year because some days we'd spend the whole day together at the Qwikpick, which is air-conditioned.

When school started it turned out we only had one class together, but thank goodness we still had the same lunch period, and of course we still had the Qwikpick after school.

SECTION III
Our Headquarters

Our headquarters are in the Qwikpick break room, which is upstairs and practically as big as my whole trailer.

This is a great place to hang out, because:

(a) No one actually uses it to take a break, because they're not allowed to smoke in it. They all go out back and smoke on their breaks. (Yes, my parents both smoke even though they keep trying to quit.)

(b) Larry the manager--my parents' boss--lets us have leftover biscuits, expired beef jerky, Halloween candy that didn't sell, and free drinks as long as we bring our own cups and don't use the store's Styrofoam cups. Cups are inventory, he says, but soda is just sugar water.

Larry used to own the
Qwikpick back when it was called
Middle Earth Mini-Mart & Subs.
I think it was his parents' store
a long time ago, but he had to
sell it to the Qwikpick chain.
They made him move out of the
upstairs room where he used to
live--which is now our break
room--but they let him stay as
the manager, so the place is
still a bit weird. Which is good,
because the other Qwikpicks are
all new and boring, according to
my dad. I guess most Qwikpicks
have all the same junk food,
but Larry orders weird stuff
like ketchup-flavored potato
chips and Bit-O-Honey bars. Plus
the Qwikpick has the largest
selection of pork rinds in the
world. I've never eaten one.
Larry says they're gross but they
sell. He's a nice guy, but my dad
says he has a drinking problem.

(c) When Larry moved out, he
    left a bunch of old books, a
    Lava lamp, the aforementioned
    broken TV, a VCR that doesn't
    rewind, a record player with
    a bunch of cool old records,
    and big speakers, which Larry
    had painted the words Positive
    Energy on.

(d) There's a box of old videotapes
    left over from when the
    Qwikpick used to rent movies.
    After they stopped renting
    movies, they sold them for a
    dollar each. The ones that are
    left are the ones no one wanted
    for a dollar. I've watched
    all of them. My favorites are
    a kung-fu vampire movie, a
    musical where Fred Astaire
    plays a really old college
    student, and The Princess
    Bride, which I can't believe
    no one bought for a dollar,
    because it's the funniest movie
    I've ever seen.

(e) Dave's brothers are not here.
Dave says it's better to watch
just channel seven or even
kung-fu vampires than to watch
cable at his house, where his
brothers hog the TV and act like
jerks all day.

(f) Marilla's sister is not here.
Marilla says she's a worse TV hog
than Dave's brothers! She wrote
this poem about her:

Neveah is my sister
She sits there like a blister
Watching TV nonstop
One day she'll pop
And I'll have to clean the carpet.

(g) There's nothing to do at my
place and it's too small anyway.

(h) If Dave brings a note from
home, the bus driver will drop
him off at our stop and we can
hang out at the Qwikpick until
Dave's mom gets off work at 4:45
and picks him up.

(i) Out back there's a space about a
    foot wide between the Dumpster
    and the back of the Qwikpick.
    We take turns seeing who can
    throw a football through it
    without touching the wall or
    the Dumpster. Actually, only
    Dave and I do this. Marilla
    thinks it's dumb.

(j) Marilla says the whole upstairs
    at the Qwikpick is hau nted.
    She says that one day while she
    was waiting for me and Dave, a
    closet door opened and a ball
    rolled out. (I've never seen
    anything like that and I'm
    here a lot more than she is.)

UNOFFICIAL personal note

The truth is that I end up at the Qwikpick by myself a lot. Of course, I was always here by myself before Marilla moved to Crab Creek Estates and Dave started coming over. But even now, it's not like they can come over every day. But I still like it better at the Qwikpick than at home. Plus now I have my typewriter and stuff in the break room.

Sometimes I do my homework here and watch TV until my parents' shift is over, then we all walk up to the trailer together.

SECTION IV
We Learn About
the Sludge Fountain

We held several meetings at the Qwikpick to try to figure out where to go on Christmas Day, but we could never think of anything good enough.

Mostly, the meetings were Marilla driving herself crazy trying to think of something while Dave and I played penny basketball.

We are probably the two best penny basketball players in the world, but we had to stop playing at school because of our weird teacher Mr. Michaels, who came by one day and made us stop. He says playing games with money looks like gambling. That's crazy, plus it's just a penny!

HOW TO PLAY PENNY BASKETBALL
By DAVE

PLAYER 1   PLAYER 2

1

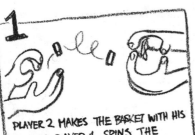

PLAYER 2 MAKES THE BASKET WITH HIS HANDS. PLAYER 1 SPINS THE PENNY TOWARD THE BASKET.

2

BEFORE SHOOTING, PLAYER 1 HAS TO CATCH the SPINNING PENNY WITH HIS THUMBS.

3 PLAYER 1 TRIES TO SHOOT THE PENNY INTO THE BASKET with HIS THUMB

IF HE MAKES IT, HE GETS 2 POINTS.
IF HE MISSES, HE DOESN'T.
EITHER WAY, PLAYER 2 THEN GETS HIS TURN.

UNOFFICIAL personal note

But since Dave is the number-one rule-follower of all time, we stopped playing. Marilla says we should still play, because it's not a sin to play penny basketball. But Dave said it's a sin to break a rule. But Marilla says God's Rules are the only rules that matter and there's no way God would bother making a rule against penny basketball.

Anyway, we never thought of anything to do for our adventure, and soon there were only a couple of school days left before Christmas, and Marilla said we absolutely had to make a decision at lunch the next day.

The next day at lunch we had to whisper about it, because we had decided to keep it a total secret from everybody. But we didn't really have any new ideas, so there wasn't much to whisper about.

"I guess we'll have to go see the banana puree," said Marilla.

"Or we could just forget it," said Dave.

But then, right after lunch, it happened! We found out about the totally perfect thing that we could do on Christmas. Marilla wants me to put that she was the one who realized it would be perfect. It's true. Dave and I never would have thought of it, and if we had thought of it, we would have thought it was a terrible idea.

It happened in Civics, the only ← class the three of us have together. It's also If you don't have Civics at your the best school, you're missing out, because class because it is fifty times better than a I sit behind regular history class. Marilla.

Our teacher Mr. Wayne is obsessed with the news. Every day, each kid is supposed to bring in a piece of news and read it to the class. Usually this takes up most of the class period and we never get around to opening our textbooks. If you bring in enough news, you get an automatic A with no studying. But a lot of the kids don't do it.

I never used to pay attention to the news, but now every morning I turn on the radio and listen to the BBC World News, which is played on the college radio station from the next county. Everybody has cool accents because the BBC News is from England.

Anyway, that same day we were sitting in class when one of the other kids, Dwayne Meyerhoffer, read a piece of news that he had clipped from the newspaper. I asked Dwayne to give me the article.

LOCAL NEWS

MAJOR SEWER UPGRADE READY IN CRICKENBURG

By Tom Angleberger

Update

CRICKENBURG—The $12-million upgrade to Crickenburg's wastewater treatment plants is ready.

On January 2, the new aeration system will begin operation, expanding the town's sewerage capacity to 20 million gallons of sewage per day.

Recent residential and industrial growth necessitated the expansion, said Mayor Roger Linkous. He said the improvements were paid for with state grants and an $8-million bond.

Plant manager Fred Swenson said that after employees return from their New Year's Day holiday they will begin the process of diverting the sewage into the new aeration facility.

The new equipment will replace the antiquated sludge fountain, which has been in use since the plant was build in 1962.

I still don't know what some of the words mean, so don't worry about them. The important part is the last sentence anyway.

A couple of kids said "Ewww!" and "Barf" and stuff like that, but Mr. Wayne said it was an important story.

He started to talk about how the town needed a bigger sewer system because of all the new houses and stores being developed around here. Development can be both good and bad, he said, but that's not what my father says.

My father says that rich people are going to develop the h-e-double-l out of this town. It won't be long, he says, before there's not a single blade of grass left around here and they tear down the Qwikpick and kick everybody out of the trailer park to put in a bigger Wal-Mart.

Mr. Wayne didn't say any of those things, but he did talk for a long time.

Then I realized that Marilla was passing me a note.

Whenever I get a note from Marilla, I always hope it's going to be the big one where she says she likes me. It wasn't.

The note said: <u>Sludge Fountain!!!</u>

I leaned forward and whispered to Marilla, "What is a sludge fountain?"

She turned around and whispered, "I don't know, Lyle, but I know how we can find out."

Mr. Wayne told us to be quiet.

SECTION V
The Debate

These are the minutes of the meeting held after school that same day while we were waiting for the bus. (As best as I can remember.)

Dave couldn't come over to the Qwikpick that afternoon, so we had to talk about it in the hall. The hall is so noisy after school that nobody could hear us.

Marilla: Did you hear that about the sludge fountain, Dave? We've got to go see that!

Dave: No thanks.

Marilla: What do you mean?

Dave: I mean, no way. Who wants to see sludge? What is sludge anyway? Isn't it just poop? And what's a sludge fountain? Does it shoot poop into the air?

Marilla: I don't know, Dave, that's
         why I want to go see it. Did
         you listen to that story?
         They're going to turn it off
         right after New Year's Day.
         If we go on Christmas, we
         could be almost the last
         people to ever see it.

Dave: But no one wants to see it.

Marilla: I do and Lyle does. Right,
         Lyle?

Lyle: Totally.

Dave: Are you serious?

Lyle: Yeah.

Marilla: C'mon, man, this is our one
         chance to go out and do
         something big without our
         parents! I never get to
         do anything without my
         parents.

UNOFFICIAL personal note

Okay, obviously I didn't totally want to see poop. But I did totally want to do something other than hang around the trailer park all day. The thing I wanted to do most was spend a whole day with Dave and Marilla.

See, they're both in band and they've always got stories about what happened at band practice or on trips to march in parades. Meanwhile, I'm in Rotation. Rotation is a bunch of different classes, like Money Matters and Fun with Numbers, for people who didn't sign up for band, home ec., or industrial arts. Rotation classes never go anywhere and nobody ever has a great story about something that happened in Rotation.

So there was no way I was going to sit at home while they went off exploring without me. This was probably going to be the most interesting thing that would happen to us all year and I had to be part of it no matter what.

Would I have gone even if I had known what was going to happen to me? Yes.

So that's why I said totally.

Dave: Me neither, that's why I want to
      do something good.

Marilla: This is good! We'll be the
         only kids who have ever seen
         it.

Dave: I don't want to get in trouble.

Marilla: Isn't it worth taking a tiny
         risk of getting in trouble to
         do something incredible?

Dave: Is smelling poop incredible?
      I didn't know that. Excuse
      me while I go to the teachers'
      lounge bathroom and have an
      incredible experience.

Marilla: All right, let's just take a
         vote.

Lyle: All in favor of going to the
      poop fountain on Christmas Day,
      say <u>aye</u>.

Marilla: Aye.

Lyle: Aye.

Dave: Aye.

UNOFFICIAL SECTION V and a half
The Great Origami Pegasus Disaster

You know why I said yes to the poop fountain, but why on earth did Dave say yes?

I'll tell you why. Dave was going to do whatever Marilla wanted just like I was and for the same reason.

See, we've never ever talked about it, but I am sure that Dave likes Marilla just as much as I do. I'm sure he guesses I like her too, but like I said, we've never said anything about it to each other and never, ever to Marilla.

So, now that you understand about that, you can understand about the Great Origami Pegasus Disaster.

What happened is we got this book called Expert Origami from the county library bookmobile some time around Thanksgiving. Origami is the Japanese art of folding things out of a single piece of paper with no scissors or glue. I had done cranes and boats and stuff before, but this book was really cool because it had all kinds of weird animals.

Marilla wasn't interested, but Dave and I started a sort of competition to make the hardest ones. We have competitions over almost everything. Up 'til then the biggest one had been language arts class. Our teacher gives out snack packs of Cheetos if you can answer bonus questions. Even though we have the class at different times, we are both trying to win the most Cheetos. Current score: Lyle 4, Dave 6. Luckily, Marilla has a different teacher, because I think she'd be beating us both. She actually likes language arts class.

Anyway, Dave and I got started on the origami. We made a vulture, a dolphin, a reindeer, a dinosaur, and a rhinoceros. (In my opinion, Dave's rhinoceros was a little squished-looking, but basically the competition was a tie up to then.)

Then we got to the last one, which was the Pegasus, which is a horse with wings. The thing is impossible. It is a total rip-off. You follow the instructions through like thirty-four steps and all of a sudden there's this funky zigzag arrow and on the next page it has turned from a lump of paper into a horse with wings.

I tried it about five times and all I got was scrunched-up paper wads with four little horse legs sticking out. I gave up and I thought Dave had too.

Then one day he shows up at lunch and he pulls out the Pegasus. I couldn't believe it. It looked just as good as the photo in the book and he had even folded it from real origami paper. I told him he'd done a great job and he told me how did it.

That wouldn't have been so bad if that had been all.

But then Marilla sits down and she says it's awesome and he shows her how it stands up and how you can fluff out the wings. She says it's the coolest thing she's ever seen and he gives it to her and later she tapes it to the inside of her locker. It's still there!

Any way you look at it, that's the biggest origami-related disaster in the history of the world. Of course Dave doesn't call it a disaster, he probably calls it the Great Origami Pegasus Triumph.

My SAD PEGASUS

Does this look like
a Pegasus to you?

Answer: NO!

SECTION VI
Planning Session

On the day that school let out at noon for Christmas break, we all took the bus back to Crab Creek Estates and then walked over to the Qwikpick.

I got out our three plastic cups so that we could all have a drink. Marilla got a Mountain Dew and I got a Mr. Pibb and Dave had water. (Dave claims that he never drinks soda. He claims that he prefers plain water. I think that's crazy.)

We went on up to the break room and there was a few minutes of hubbub because Dave saw the mouse that lives in the sofa. We're always trying to catch it to take it outside so it doesn't get caught in one of the mousetraps Larry has in the stockroom. But we didn't catch it this time either, so we got ready for our planning session.

Marilla turned on the Lava lamp,

which always takes forever to warm up.
I turned on Larry's positive energy
stereo and played one of his old
records that I like, by this rock
band called Electric Light Orchestra.
What's cool is that me, Dave, and
Marilla are the only kids in the
whole school who have ever heard of
them and they're awesome.

Dave had gotten a map from his
mom's real estate office and it showed
that the treatment plant was located
very near Crab Creek, which was an
ugly ditch that carried a little bit
of water that ran out of the downtown
area. As far as I knew there were
no crabs in it, but I had never really
looked at it much. It wasn't a cool
creek, it was just kind of a muddy
dribble full of trash that went
through a culvert under South Franklin
Street about half a mile from the
trailer park.

The sewage treatment plant was on
Crab Creek Road, which isn't that far

from the Crab Creek Estates Trailer
Park, as you might guess. However, it's
a pretty long way down Crab Creek
Road to the plant. Dave figured the
round trip would be about six miles,
which wouldn't have been too bad on
our bikes.

But the only way to get to Crab
Creek Road by bike is to ride down
South Franklin Street. Every kid in
Crickenburg knows that riding your
bike on South Franklin Street is the
number-one way to have a cop drive by
and yell at you.

It isn't our fault that South
Franklin Street has become an
eight-lane traff ic fiasco of crazed
Wal-Mart shoppers! If they want to
yell at someone, they should yell at
the Wal-Mart shoppers, not kids
riding their bikes.

So we made the decision to walk
there instead. Dave looked at the

map and said it wouldn't be so far if
we cut across the fields behind the
trailer park.

Crab Creek Estates is right on the
edge of Crickenburg, and so if you go
to the back row of trailers, you can
see right into a farm.

"I guess we can't do that, though,"
said Dave, "because it would be
trespassing."

"It's no problem, I've been back
in those fields before," I told Dave.
"There's nobody around. Just cows and
a lot of cow pies. If you walk up the
hill a bit, you can see Wal-Mart and
Taco Bell by the bypass, so I guess you
could walk up that way. But I didn't
know you could go down to Crab Creek."

"It looks that way on the map," he
said. "It should only be about three
miles there and back."

That's about all the planning we
did. Marilla wants me to mention that

we played Ms. Pac-Man after that, because that was the day she got her new all-time high score of 49,790.

Maybe we should have done some more planning instead.

Marilla's high score

SECTION VII
Pre-Adventure Preparations
on Christmas morning

Like I said, since my parents were both going to be working Christmas morning, we opened our presents on Christmas Eve. I got some clothes, a new Pinkwater book I wanted called Lizard Music, and this typewriter.

The more I've been thinking about it, the more I'm glad my parents didn't spend a lot of money on a computer. It always makes me feel guilty when my parents spend money on me. There are some kids at school who are all braggy about getting their parents to buy them something expensive, but don't they realize that their parents had to work for that money? It's not free money.

Like last Christmas I did get the new fifteen-speed bike that I asked for. It cost $129. Then a couple of weeks later my father started having one of his big things about how we were never going to pay off the credit cards and his student loans from when he was in college but didn't finish.

Whenever Dad's student loans come up it's always bad, he usually ends up shouting and having to leave the house for a long time and when he comes back he always says he's sorry he got mad but it just shows how I can't screw up like he did.

my trailer

After the presents, my parents went to bed and got up at four in the morning to go to the Qwikpick. I almost went crazy waiting until nine, when Dave and Marilla were supposed to get there.

We had decided not to meet at the Qwikpick this time, since we were trying to limit possible adult interference. Marilla said that she would under no conditions lie to her parents or to my parents, so we had better be careful that no one asked her any questions.

So we met at my trailer.

I'll admit that I had the secret hope that Dave wouldn't show up, so that Marilla and I would end up spending the day together. I have a bad feeling that he probably hoped I wouldn't be able to go too.

Anyway, this time it was a good thing we were all there, because I think that if it was just two of us, we would have chickened out and we probably would have had just a normal boring day.

Dave sometimes says weird stuff like this that makes absolutely no sense to anybody but he thinks it's funny. Apparently it's from an old-time song or something.

Dave knocked on my door and shouted, "Open the door, Richard!"

I let him in. Marilla was already there and the three of us toasted frozen waffles and ate them with peanut butter. Then we made peanut butter and jelly sandwiches to take with us.

"Before we start, I want to get a picture of all three of us," said Marilla.

Even though her parents don't celebrate Christmas or birthdays, Marilla had told me that she and her sister usually get some kind of new toy every year around this time, so that they don't feel left out. This year she got a camera.

I don't think it was quite as nice as the one she wanted, but it was still really cool and must have cost her parents a lot.

She put her new camera on the kitchen counter and turned on the timer function. We all stood together holding up our pennies until the camera flashed. Dave had suggested that we throw pennies into the poop fountain for good luck. Marilla planned to take pictures of that as well. Unfortunately, Marilla was still learning how to use the camera, so the picture is of our kitchen cabinets.

our kitchen cabinets

We got our coats on and Marilla went
through this elaborate process of tying
her hair up. She has really long black
hair, way down past her shoulders. It
is always getting into stuff, like gravy
and ketchup.

"Man, if my hair dips down into
that poop fountain and gets poop on
it, then you guys will have to just
shave it all off," she said with a
shiver.

"Actually," said Dave, who often
starts sentences with that word,
"I read this story once about a princess
whose hair accidentally dipped into
a magic fountain and it turned to
pure gold."

"Great," said Marilla, "my hair will
turn to pure poop!"

You should know that we cracked
up each time any of us said the word
poop. Yeah, it's kind of second-grade,
I know, but once the word poop has
been said fifty times, the fifty-first
time is twice as funny. Try it.

Marilla wants me to put that she never uses that other word that means the same thing but is a bad word. How can you have two words that mean the same thing but one of them is a bad word and the other one isn't? I don't know, but none of us say that other one.

We disagree on whether <u>turd</u> is a bad word. Marilla and I say no, but Dave says a teacher told him it was.

She looked very cute like this.

Anyway, once Marilla had her hair all tied up and stuck under her Carolina Mudcats baseball cap, it didn't seem likely to get in the fountain.

I started to worry that my glasses might fall in. They are always sliding down my nose because the lenses are very thick and heavy.

I decided to tie them around my neck with a shoelace just in case. I imagine I looked even more like a goober, but the others didn't say anything.

"Geez, guys, how close were you planning to get to the poop anyway?"

Dave asked. "I thought we were going to peek at the poop from a distance."

"I'm not taking any chances," said Marilla. "Who knows how far that poop shoots through the air."

We laughed at this too, but we shouldn't have. It was very prophetic.

SECTION VIII
The Journey

Time: 9:35 A.M. to 11:10 A.M.

It was a little colder than I expected. The radio said high thirties, but the temperature always seems lower in Crickenburg, because of the mountains, I guess.

Dave had some fancy Polartec gloves he had gotten for Hanukkah, Marilla had some pink knitted mittens, and I spent most of the day with my hands in my pockets because I had lost so many pairs of gloves, my mother said she wouldn't buy me any more.

Marilla said, "H-h-have you h-h-heard of H-H-Herbert H-H-Hoover's h-h-horse?" and every time she made an "h" sound, you could see her breath.

Dave was in charge of the map. He is also the one who drew the map that is attached to this report. Dave is really good at drawing trucks, robots, and spaceships.

UNOFFICIAL personal note

Dave is always complaining that he has to take PE but can't take an art class, because he thinks he would get straight A's in art.

Frankly, I'd rather take <u>any</u> class other than PE. All I ever do there is sit around watching other kids play basketball.

When I do get to play, I spend the whole time angry because no one will throw me the ball, then in the rare event that somebody does, someone like Kevin Morris always comes over and practically tackles me to get it. This is basketball I'm talking about, not football.

My favorite PE game is crab soccer because no one can really tell if you're good at that or not. Dave agrees. Marilla is actually pretty good at basketball and she says that crab soccer is for losers. To which I say, "CRAB SOCCER IS THE SPORT OF KINGS!"

I don't see why you have to learn how to use a compass. It just points north, doesn't it?

Anyway, Dave opened up the map and got out a compass.

"Oh good grief, let's get moving," said Marilla. "What do you need to look at that for? We know how to get started at least."

"A good orienteer looks at his map before he gets lost so that he doesn't get lost," said Dave. Dave went to an outdoor camp last summer and learned how to use a compass.

"The first thing to do is to go to the back of the trailer park and climb over the fence into the cow pasture," said Dave.

I very nearly said "DUH!" But I didn't because I hate it when people say that. But seriously, sometimes Dave acts like I'm some sort of idiot.

We ended up crawling under the fence, which was barbed wire. The field is huge. I'm not talking about a football field, I'm talking about something a hundred times that size. You can't even tell how big it is exactly because of hills and stuff. But it's really big.

"Where's the cows?" asked Dave.

"I think the farmer moved them out. My dad says that someone bought all this and is going to build town houses on it," I said.

UNOFFICIAL personal note

Actually, my dad had said a lot more than that. He said that once the town houses were built, our trailer park wouldn't last long. The people in the town houses would say that we were bringing down their property values. He gets really mad about this stuff. If it ever really happens, I think he'll bust a blood vessel in his brain.

"Well, they left plenty of cow poop behind," said Marilla, poking a cow pile with her foot. "Look how dry this is. It's like it turns into paper on top."

"That's disgusting," said Dave. However, he and I did have to confirm that she was correct. The top of a cow pile does turn into paper.

We started walking and went up a small hill. When we got to the top, we turned around and could see a long ways away.

"See, Dave? You can actually see the Wal-Mart from here and then over there's the top of the Taco Bell sign. I bet you can just go right across the field to get there."

"Yeah, I know," he said. "Maybe we can go there after we're done."

"Ug," I said. "Will we really want to eat a burrito after seeing all that poop?"

"Well, all food is just pre-poop, but burritos are more pre-poop than anything," said Marilla. That doesn't look so funny now that I've typed it out, but when she said it, we all just about busted a gut.

SECTION IX
The Hill Hop, or,
The Bulldozer Incident

We kept walking and following Dave's directions. It was weird because we were walking right behind the houses in the fancy new place called Mountain View Pointe. Marilla says that's a stupid name because there's hardly any places around here where you can't see a mountain. Plus they spelled point wrong.

Dave said his mother, who is a Realtor in case you forgot, sold one of those houses and made a commission of $40,000.

UNOFFICIAL personal note

That's more money than either of my
parents makes in a whole year, even with
all the extra shifts and stuff. It's not that
Dave is bragging about having more money
than us, it's more like he's totally unaware
of it. He's never a jerk about having money,
he just never seems to realize that I don't.
Like one time I wore this really cool shirt
with an alligator on it and it said "Florida
Everglades." And Dave goes, "Oh, have you
been to the Everglades, isn't it awesome?"
That was embarrassing, because obviously
I haven't been to the Everglades. I've only
been out of the state a couple of times and
that was just to go to West Virginia, and I
certainly wouldn't buy a T-shirt there. The
shirt came from the thrift store and I just
bought it because I liked the alligator, but
now I don't wear it anymore. But like I said,
Dave isn't a jerk, he's just not very good at
avoiding the subject, which is what I try to
do at all times.

It felt good to be walking around
the fields with Marilla and Dave
even if it was cold. I think we were
all glad we were taking a shortcut
instead of just riding our bikes down
South Franklin Street. This made it
more of an adventure, like that movie
The Goonies or Stand by Me, or even in
Lord of the Rings where they have to
walk and walk and walk through the
mountains.

But instead of wild adv entures
like in those stories, we just ran
into a lot of cow pies.

"This is awesome," I said.
"Definitely," said Marilla.

UNOFFICIAL personal note

It really was awesome. I was so glad there
weren't any other kids there to spoil it. Me
and Dave and Marilla have a great time at the
Qwikpick, but at school it never works out so
good. There's always Elizabeth or one of the other
nerd guys or even Jeremy around. Sometimes I
feel like I'm competing with those other kids to get
Dave and Marilla to notice me.

Like when we took our field trip to Monticello,
which is Thomas Jefferson's house, back in
September. Everybody paired up to get a bus
seat partner. Marilla sat with Elizabeth, of
course. I expected that. But Dave sat with Mark.
Apparently they always sit together on band
trips.

Great, so I ended up sitting with this scary
guy Dakota Martin, and he spent the whole time
listening to his headphones and drawing on his
leg with a pen. No wonder nobody wanted to sit
with him.

I did get to sit near Dave and Marilla, but
every time I would try to turn around to talk

to them, Mr. Michaels would tell me to sit down. If Mr. Michaels wanted to do something useful, why didn't he stop Jeremy from spending eighty-five dollars at the gift shop? What a lousy trip.

Anyway I was glad it was just the three of us walking through the fields.

After a while we had to crawl under another barbed wire fence to get into the next field. This one was smaller and there were hundreds of rotted, frozen pumpkins on the ground.

"You know what this is?" I said. "This is Farmer Don's Pick Your Own Pumpkin Patch!"

This is where my family always gets a pumpkin for Halloween even though they cost more than at Food Lion. My dad thinks Farmer Don is the greatest guy in the world, because he is surrounded by town houses but he keeps on growing pumpkins.

But Dave pointed to these stakes that were in the ground with pink ribbons tied to them. He said those mean that the field has been mapped out and is probably going to get houses built on it.

"I guess Farmer Don sold out," said Dave.

"No way," I said. "Farmer Don would never sell out--maybe someone forced him to give it up."

"Maybe," said Dave. "But the builders sometimes offer a ton of money."

Well, you can't convince Dave of anything, but I still believe Farmer Don would never have sold out.

We walked up a long hill to get through the pumpkin patch, and even though it was cold, we were starting to get hot under our coats and hats.

When we got to the top of the hill and looked down, we saw a huge construction site for new town houses.

the construction site

There was no grass anywhere, just frozen dirt and huge rocks and bulldozers and stuff everywhere, but because it was Christmas nobody was around to see us, so instead of going arou nd, we just walked right through. That's when the Bulldozer Incident happened.

The three of us have agreed to record the details of the Bulldozer Incident. Dave wants it in writing to prove that he is not guilty of anything. Marilla and I wanted to write it down because it was fun.

We came to a place where a bunch of vehicles were parked.

Or it could have been if Dave hadn't ruined it.

At first I was embarrassed to climb on them in case Marilla thought it was dumb, but then she was actually the first one to climb on.

Marilla climbed up on a big bulldozer. I got on one of those things that has a big scoop on the end of this big crane arm thing. It was totally cool--there were so many levers and knobs and things to control the scoops. I have always wanted to dig a big hole with one of these things.

bulldozer-type thing

"Guys, get down, are you crazy!" Dave yelled.

"What's the problem?" said Marilla.

"You're not supposed to climb on those," Dave said. "C'mon!"

"I don't see any signs about it," I said.

"It's an unwritten rule," he said.

Man, if you have to follow all the written rules and all the unwritten rules, what's left?

"We're not hurting anything," said Marilla. "Come up here and see this. It's awesome."

"No way," said Dave. "You guys are going to get us all in big trouble."

That's when I noticed the keys.

"Hey, Marilla, the keys are still in this one," I yelled, and she jumped off the bulldozer and climbed up next to me.

"Should we turn it on?" I asked. (Please note I didn't actually turn it on, I just asked the question.)

"I'm going home," said Dave, and he

turned around and started walking
back.

"Man, what is his major malfunction?"
muttered Marilla. And then she yelled,
"Dave, get back here!"

He kept walking. Marilla and I
glanced at each other and she rolled
her eyes. We had to jump down and
chase him.

"All right, Dave, c'mon, we won't mess
with the stuff anym ore," said Marilla.

"Forget it, I'm going home," he said.

"You mean you're not going to the poop
fountain?" I asked.

"No, you guys are just going to get
me in trouble."

"Aaarg!" shouted Marilla. "Would you
at least stop walking the wrong way
while we talk about this?"

Dave stopped. When Marilla shouts,
which doesn't happen hardly ever, you
pretty much have to do what she says.

"Look," said Marilla, "I'm sorry
about the bulldozer. We won't do

I hated to admit it, but it was true and I also figured it would help him to change his mind. I could tell that if he gave up, Marilla and I probably would too. And then we'd all be mad and the day would be a waste.

anything else like that. We'll be extra-super-careful."

"Plus, we need you and your map to find the place," I said.

"All right," he said finally, "but seriously, you guys have got to chill out and not do anything else like that."

We agreed and we all turned around and walked back past the bulldozers without touching them.

I probably wouldn't have had the nerve to start one up anyway. I'm not as bad as Dave, but I'm mostly a rule-follower too.

On the other side of the construction
we came to a whole ton of brambles. It
was like a jungle and what was weird
was there were a million Wal-Mart bags
in there. They must have blown all the
way across the fields and gotten stuck.

"Sorry, guys," said Dave, "these
brambles weren't on the map."

I found a big stick and tried to
knock the brambles down in front of us,
but we still got our pants caught on
the little thorns a lot.

"My mother is going to kill me if my
coat gets ripped," said Marilla. She took
it off and held it up over her head as
we struggled through the thorns.

After about five minutes of this, the
brambles thinned out and then it was
mostly regular bushes and then a lot of
trees. It wasn't like a beautiful
forest, though, because the trees
weren't that old and there were lots
more plastic bags.

"Well, now I'm freezing again," said
Marilla, putting her coat back on.

Even though I was sweating under my coat, my hands were frozen. "Are we ever going to get there?" I asked.

"The map shows we've gone at least halfway," said Dave.

"Only halfway? We've been walking for hours!"

"Actually only forty-eight minutes," said Dave, looking at his watch.

Finally, we got to a place that was more like a real forest, so it was pretty neat.

Even though we live near a national forest and all these mountains, I never get to go hiking in the woods. My parents just don't have the energy when they get a day off. And I got drummed out of the Cub Scouts pretty quick. A lot of those kids were okay at school, but get a bunch of them together in a church basement without enough adult supervision and ... well, let's just say I was lucky to get out alive! But I did win the pinewood derby, so eat my dust, weeblos!

We had been walking downhill for a while. All of a sudden, it got really steep. Down at the bottom we could see a creek, maybe even Crab Creek.

"That looks pretty slippery," I said. "There are dead leaves everywhere."

"Don't worry," said Dave, "I learned how to do the Hill Hop at camp. You go down sideways."

All of a sudden Dave hurled himself down the hill and he really did go sideways. Kind of jum ping and falling, faster and faster until just when it looked like he was about to die, he would grab a tree and swing around the trunk to slow down.

"C'mon, Jaybees!" he shouted.

So Marilla and I tried it too.

What happens is you get going so fast because of the hill, then when you put your feet down, that sort of throws you into the air. It's too

That's another of his weird sayings that nobody else understands.

HILL HOPPING

GO SIDEWAYS

LAND + JUMP

OH NO! BETTER GRAB A TREE

complicated to explain, so Dave has
drawn an instructional diagram. It
was really fun even though the whole
time I thought I was going to break my
ankle.

Marilla forgot that we were sneaking
around and let out a big whoop. I wanted
to whoop too. I never got going as fast
as Dave did, but one time I think I was
about six feet in the air. Then when
I landed, I slipped on the leaves and
slid halfway down the hill on my back.

"How on earth are we going to get
back up that hill?" Marilla asked
when we all got to the bottom. It was a
mighty good question.

"And where do we go now?" I asked,
pointing to the creek. "That's bigger
than I expected. I don't think I can
jump across."

"You know what's weird?" said Dave.
"According to the map, this has got to
be Crab Creek."

"But Crab Creek's just a tiny trickle,"
said Marilla. "This is a lot of water."

"I can think of only one explanation," said Dave.

"What's that?" I said, although I couldn't see that it mattered.

"Well, think about it. We're now downstream from the poop plant."

"Are you saying--"

"Yes, this water is what comes out of the poop plant after they've taken out the poop."

"I'm going to be sick," I said.

We all three began sniffing and backing away from the water.

"I'm sure it's clean," said Dave. "I mean, there must be a law that says it can't have any poop left in it."

"Why don't you drink some, then?" Marilla said.

Marilla says that looking back on it now, it's hard to believe we were so grossed out by cleaned water. That was nothing compared to what was ahead.

SECTION X
The Sneak-in

Since we were downstream from the plant, Dave said all we had to do was walk upstream to get to it.

We had only gone about a hundred yards when a huge concrete pipe appeared out of the ground. Just as Dave had said, a ton of water was coming out of the pipe and going into the creek. Ahead of the pipe, the creek was just a tiny little stream that we easily jumped over.

From here we could see that the place was surrounded by a tall chain-link fence.

"Well, at least it doesn't have barbed wire on top of it," I said.

I climbed a little way up to test it out.

"Oh yeah, we can climb this no problem," I said.

Neither Dave nor Marilla started climbing, though.

I didn't see how that mattered, but it was obvious they weren't going to climb over the fence. Man, it's not easy to sneak into a poop plant with the number-one rule-follower of all time.

"I thought we were going to be super-extra-careful not to break any rules," said Dave. "Maybe we can find a gate or something."

"Yeah," said Marilla. "That way, if we get caught and they ask us how we got in, we won't have to say we climbed over the fence."

We followed the fence for a little ways and, at last, we came to Crab Creek Road. It ran right into the plant through an OPEN GATE! We just walked right in!

"How can they even say we're trespassing?" said Marilla. "We just walked through an open gate."

This was pretty shaky logic, but me and Dave didn't argue.

the entrance

"Look," said Dave, "the parking lot's empty."

He was right. There were spaces for about ten cars outside of a two-story brick building.

"That must be the command center," said Dave.

"Does a poop plant need a command center?" I asked.

"Well, someone has to turn the poop fountain on and off," Dave said.

As it turned out, we learned the hard way that the poop fountain turns on and off by itself.

the command center

SECTION XI
The Smell

"Uh, guys, do you smell something?" Marilla asked.

Yes, we did smell something.

It was still faint here in the parking lot, but it was all around us. It didn't smell exactly like poop, but you knew it had to be some sort of poop by-product.

Beyond the alleged command center, there was a cluster of strangely shaped big concrete buildings. One of them was one story high, but maybe fifty yards long. Another, which looked like a tower with a dome on top, had a sign on it that said "Methane Release Unit." So far it was weird and gross, but definitely not worth coming all this way for.

I was surprised to see that there was grass and bushes and mulch beds around. Why bother trying to make a poop plant look nice?

As we walked between the buildings, there was a du ll roaring sound under the ground. There must have been pipes and things buried.

"You know, that newspaper article was talking about millions of gallons of sewage," said Dave. "That's a lot of poop. There must be like a whole river of it under our feet."

"Yeah, I can smell it," said Marilla.

I've thought a lot about this, and it would be wrong to say the smell was getting worse. It's just that it was getting heavier and thicker. It seemed like you could reach out and touch it.

Afterward, we all agre ed that it felt like we could actually feel the stink particles sticking to our clothes. Dave says he thought it would gradually build up until we'd be able to peel them off like a Fruit Roll-Up. That didn't happen, of course, but that is what it felt like.

We got to the end of the long short building and turned the corner. And there it was.

The poop fountain!

It had to be. It looked like a huge, overgrown public fountain in a big city.

UNOFFICIAL personal note

Actually, I've never been to a big city, but Dave goes to Chicago with his family every year and he says they have big fountains like this, but with clean water, of course. When we get to the eighth grade we're going to take a field trip to Washington, D.C.—if we sell enough candy bars— so maybe we'll see one then. But I bet it won't be as big as the poop fountain.

It was a big rectangular pool, about
the size of the library at school. It was
surrounded by a low concrete wall about
three feet high. In the middle of it was
this big concrete cube that was about
thirty feet high. Near the top it had
these big slits.

We could tell that poop came out of
the slits because there were big dark
stains splattered underneath each one.

"It's not on," Marilla moaned. "It's not
running!"

"Don't tell me they already shut it
down," I said.

"I wonder if it's empty," said Dave,
and he started to walk toward it. He
took a couple of steps and turned around
with his hand over his nose.

"This is where the smell is coming
from!"

He took another step toward the edge,
then came running back. "It's not empty.
It's like a giant swimming pool of BM.
The stink almost killed me!"

We all put our shirts over our noses
and tried to walk forward.

Every breath was like swallowing poison. It was like there was a poop mist and every time you inhaled, you let more and more into your lungs and eventually you'd drown in it.

We held our noses, but it came in through our mouths. We didn't drown, but I gagged a lot and so did the others.

The problem with typing this up is that you won't be able to smell what we smelled, so you'll never really know what it was like.

However, Marilla had a great idea about how to better record the smell: poetry. She says that poets can make you feel things that regular writers can't. She said that poets can make a picture with words, so maybe we can make a smell with words.

So we have all written haikus to help describe the smell experience. If you don't know what a haiku is, it's a Japanese kind of poem that Mrs. Petras taught us earlier this year. The words

don't have to rhyme, but they do have to
have the right number of syllables. Five
for the first line, seven for the second
line, and five for the last line. Dave's
doesn't have exactly the right number
of syllables, but he said he likes it the
way it is.

"ODE TO AN ODOR"
BY LYLE

Like a butterfly
On the breeze, the stink flies in
To my brain, then dies

"After the Fountain"

by Marilla

Bacon fat farts and
Fresh barf and dead rodents will
Smell good to me now

SECTION XII
Sunken "Treasure"

But poetry was not on our minds at that moment. In fact I was wondering if you could get seriously ill from breathing in this stuff.

"Let's just go," I said through my shirt. "It's not even turned on."

"We might as well take a look," said Marilla. "We came all this way."

"What's to see?" I asked.

Actually, what we saw was just plain weird. The fountain seemed to be about half full of pure liquid chocolate. Maybe a little grayer than chocolate syrup, but seriously, if the smell hadn't been there, I would have thought it was chocolate.

It was getting easier to breathe. Maybe our brains were learning how to block out the smell.

"Actually," said Dave, "I do see something. It looks like a wallet."

We went up to the edge of the fountain.
There were some scraps of who-knows-what
floating on the surface of the chocolate.
One of the things floating was a wallet
just a little ways away.

"How did a wallet get in there?" asked
Marilla.

"I guess somebody flushed it," I said.
"Maybe it fell out of their pocket while
they were sitting down on the toilet."

"Wouldn't they have fished it out?"
said Dave.

"I guess it depends how much money
was in it," Marilla said.

"Maybe we should get it out," I said.
"If there's a name in it, we can give
it back and get a reward, and if there
isn't, maybe there is money in it and we
can keep it."

"Would you really want money that's
been soaking in poop for a week?" asked
Dave.

"Yes," said me and Marilla at the same
time.

"Look down there," I said. "It's like a

long net or something. They must scoop stuff out of here all the time." I walked down to where a long pole was lying against a railing. It did not have a net, but one end was extremely stained and nasty, so I figured they must use it for stirring stuff up.

"Nope, it's not a net, just a poop stirrer," said Marilla.

"Maybe you could get it under the wallet and sort of lift it out," said Dave.

I picked it up by the clean end. At least I had thought it was the clean end. Once I was actually touching it, it felt kind of greasy.

The pole was about ten feet long and it was kind of hard to use. I lifted it out over the poop water and it plopped in with a splash. One little drop came shooting back toward us. We all screamed and then started laughing, but that just made us swallow more poop air.

"Dis-gust," said Ma rilla.

I tried again, but the pole always came up short of the wallet.

"I don't think I can reach it," I said.

UNOFFICIAL personal note

Now, this is a little embarrassing, but the truth is that Dave and I are not only the shortest guys in the class, we are also shorter than most of the girls. My mother says that girls grow sooner than boys. So it is a simple fact of life that Marilla is about a foot taller than either one of us. There is no need for her to call us "shrimps."

So Marilla tried the pole and almost got the wallet on her first try.

"I just need to get a little closer," she said. She climbed up on the wall and started leaning over the poop water.

"You guys hold on to my coat. Do not let me even start to fall or I'll kill you."

"Are you crazy?" I shouted, but I knew that she had to try it. We had come all this way for a supposed adventure. Well, this was it, dangerous acrobatics above a lake of liquid human waste. She had obviously forgotten all about the promise she'd made Dave to be extra-super-careful, but I think he had too.

She got on her knees up on the wall. Me and Dave both got really good grips on her coat.

"Okay, here goes."

She stretched farther and farther out. I could feel my fingers starting to sweat and lose their grip on the coat. She was really going for it.

The pole was poking its way closer and closer. It had to be near the wallet by now, I thought. I could really feel my grip getting slippery.

"Just come back!" I hollered.

"A little more," she whispered, and wiggled forward on her knees.

"I got it!"

Somewhere beneath us I heard a loud thunk.

And then the fountain erupted.

SECTION XIII
The Sacrifice

A lot of things happened at once.

More chocolate water--this stuff looked like that dark chocolate you sometimes get at Christmas--started gushing out of the slits in the big concrete cube. I mean, it was shooting out like crazy. It really was a fountain except instead of the water going straight up in the air, it was shooting out horizontally in every direction. Including right at us!

All three of us were yelling.

Dave says his first instinct was to cover his face, and I felt that too. But we couldn't let go of Marilla's coat.

Marilla meanwhile was trying to twist around to get off the wall.

"Pull me off!" she hollered, swinging the pole wildly over our heads. There was a big fudgey blob on the end. She had gotten the wallet.

We were just starting to realize that the poop wasn't shooting out far enough to hit us, when we saw something else flying through the air.

It was Marilla's new camera. As she twisted around it came loose from her coat pocket.

Later we all agreed that we saw it clearly for just a second. Just sort of flying through space in front of a chocolaty backdrop. Then there was a plop, close enough to splash us with tiny drops of poop, and it was gone.

UNOFFICIAL personal note

I looked at Marilla and saw a million things going through her head. She'd lost her great new present. She would get in a ton of trouble and she'd never get another one. Not for years, anyway. Her parents had bought her a present they couldn't really afford and she had lost it.

I knew she was thinking all those things because that's what I would be thinking.

I saw that she was about to cry, and Marilla isn't the kind of girl who ever cries.

So that's why I did it. I didn't do it to try to impress her or to make her like me, although those would have been nice. I did it because if it had been me, I would have cried too.

I plunged my hand in after it.
When I finally felt the plastic with my
fingertips, I was in up to my shoulder.
My feet were off the ground and I found
out later that Dave and Marilla were
tugging on my pants to keep me from
falling in. I was clinging to the wall
with my other arm and trying to keep
my head out of the liquid. But the
splashing fountain was splattering my
hair with poop anyway. Some even got on
my face. It was a good thing I had tied
on my glasses with a shoelace, because
they started to slip off.

My nose was only inches away from
the sludge, but I don't remember what
the smell was like because I was thinking
that my arm was colder than it had ever
been. The poop water felt like it was
ready to turn into poop ice. So did my arm.

For a second I thought the camera was
going to be too slippery to pick up, but
my fingers closed on it and I held it in
a death grip.

Marilla and Dave were pulling me up.

Actually she said, "Oh my God," but she asked me not to write it that way because it is a sin to take the Lord's name in vain. (That change is the only lie in this whole report!)

A second later I was back on my feet.
"Oh my gosh!" said Marilla.
I held the camera out to her. She reached for it and then realized it was completely slimed up with muddy poop and drew her hand back.

I felt like maybe she was also about to hug me, maybe even kiss me, but then I realized I was just as poop-covered as the camera. So we just stood there looking at each other.

SECTION XIV
Santa Claus

"I can't be-leeeeve you did that," said Dave.

"Me neither! Thank you so much, Lyle!" said Marilla. She pulled off her scarf and used it to take the camera from me. She started wiping it down. "I hope it still works."

I started taking my coat off. Then I realized my clothes were soaked all the way through.

"Jeez, I think I'm going to freeze to death."

"Oh man, we're three miles from home, you will freeze to death," said Marilla.

"Yeah, what were you thinking?" asked Dave. "And if you do get home, how are you going to explain why you're covered in poop? Or how about the fact that you stink worse than anything your parents have ever smelled before?"

"What are we gonna do?" asked Marilla. "Lyle, I am so sorry."

"Wait a minute," said Dave, pointing. "Maybe Santa Claus will help."

"Ha, ha," I said, but he kept pointing, so I swung around and looked. There was Santa Claus.

For one split second I was like, "All right, we're saved."

It wasn't Santa, of course. It was a man in a Santa Claus hat who happened to have a beard. He wasn't overly fat and he was wearing green coveralls.

Then Marilla said, "Now we're busted."

"Oh, no!" moaned Dave as he realized the same thing. "I knew it."

I think if the guy had been wearing just the coveralls and not the hat, we would have taken off running. But for some reason the hat made us just stand there while he walked up to us.

"Merry Christmas," he said.

SECTION XV
Santa Is a Nice Guy

"We've had kids sneak in here before," he said to me, "but you're the first to go swimming."

"I had to get her camera," I said. "Are we in trouble?"

"Yes, I'd say you're in deep doo-doo," Santa said. Then he laughed this crazy hacking laugh like my mother's friend who is a chain-smoker.

"You're not going to call the police, are you?" asked Dave.

"Well, I'm sure my boss, Brenda-- she's the town manager--she would want me to take you down to the police station and file a report. She's a real stickler for regulations."

I started to feel sick, and Dave and Marilla say they did too.

I bet Dave especially was about to die since his all-time biggest fear of getting in trouble for breaking a rule was coming true.

But then Santa said, "But why bother the police? It's good to see young people interested in wastewater management. Plus I should have locked the gate, but I didn't figure anybody would come down here on Christmas Day. I just went home to have some lunch."

"Lunch?" Dave said like a zombie. We all were having trouble believing we weren't in trouble.

"Yeah, on holidays we pretty much put this place on autopilot, so I was able to have lunch with my parents."

Then he looked at me. "C'mon, buddy, let's get you cleaned up. We've got showers in the command center." As soon as Santa called me buddy, I knew we were going to be okay. He wasn't even going to yell at us.

"Wait a minute," said Dave. "You really do call it the command center?"

"You got to call it something."

SECTION XVI
The Command Center

Santa turned out to be Fred Swenson, the plant manager we had read about in the newspaper article. He was really cool. He said we should call him Freddie because nobody ever calls him Fred except the newspaper. I figure he was maybe fifty-five. Dave says he's pretty sure Freddie is a hippie. Marilla said you can't tell if someone's a hippie when they're wearing green coveralls.

While I took a shower in a locker room a lot like the one at school, Freddie showed Dave and Marilla around the command center. Dave says it had a lot of computers and poop-testing equ ipment. On a non-holiday there are five people working there, Freddie said, mostly to test water quality. Dave says that Freddie told them the water that flows into the creek is actually cleaner than the water that's already in the creek. He (Dave, not Freddie) is planning to do a science fair project about it this spring.

Also while I was gone, Marilla finished cleaning off her camera and then turned it on.

"It still works!" she hollered when I emerged from the locker room and she took a picture of me. "Holy cow, you look like the mayor of Munchkinland!"

Freddie had given me the smallest size of coveralls that they had. I had rolled the sleeves and pants up about twe nty times. Maybe I did look dumb, but it was better than wearing the poop-soaked clothes, which I had double-bagged in some trash bags Freddie gave me.

"Thanks again for saving my camera, Lyle," Marilla said.

"You don't even smell anymore," she said, laughing. I laughed too.

At this point she gave me a sort of half hug, which was pretty nice. Even though it was just a half hug, there was this little extra squeeze to it that was too quick for Dave to see, but which I will never forget. So, like I said, don't give up hope for Marilla liking me someday.

SECTION XVII
A Special Treat

"C'mon," said Dave, "we're about to go back outside. We forgot the wallet."

"That's a funny thing," said Freddie. "Like I was telling these two, we get all kinds of crazy stuff, but we don't get many wallets. I found a Molly Hatchet tape once. It's awesome; it still works!"

None of us had any idea what he was talking about.

We went back out. It seemed awful cold. The coveralls weren't warm and my hair was still kind of wet.

Freddie gave Dave some plastic gloves to put on, and Dave picked up the wallet off the ground and opened it.

"Yeah, there's about eight bucks in here and some soggy paper and some credit cards and a driver's license. The name is Murray Dillow. Huh, he lives out in Floyd County. I wonder how he flushed his wallet in Crickenburg."

"Probably at Wal-Mart," I said.

Shopping at Wal-Mart is the only reason anybody comes to Crickenburg from Floyd County or from anywhere else either.

"Do you guys want me to send it back to him or would you like to?" asked Freddie as he held out a plastic bag for Dave to drop the wallet in.

"We'll take care of it," said Marilla. "Really, we will. We won't just keep the money."

"I believe you," said Freddie, and laughed that smoker laugh again and handed her the bag. Marilla put it in her coat pocket, the one without the camera.

"Freddie," she asked, "what's going to happen to the poop fountain? Is it really being replaced?"

"Yeah. You s ee that new building over there?" he said, and pointed to the tower-looking thing we had seen earlier. "That thing is like a big Jacuzzi. You pump the sewage in, then big jets of air stir it up until the water separates from the solids."

"Ug, what are solids?" Dave asked.

"You know, the stuff that Lyle here was covered in. You have to separate the solids from the water before you can clean the water. The fountain did that too, but the new tank can handle three times as much."

"You know," he said, "besides me and a couple of the other employees, you'll probably be the last people to ever see it gush. It's been like Old Faithful all these years."

"Will you miss it?" I asked.

"Are you kidding? It's the nastiest, most disgusting thing I've seen in my whole life."

"And the smelliest," said Marilla.

"Actually, no," said Freddie. "Not the smelliest."

"What smells worse than this?" she asked.

"Follow me."

We looked nervously at each other. I didn't know if I could handle a worse smell, but none of us wanted to back out now.

We followed Freddie over to this big concrete building that said "Solids Dewatering Building."

"This is the thickening room and grit chamber," he said, pulling a keychain from his pocket. "I really don't know why I bother locking it."

He opened the door and we all staggered back. It wasn't the thick, chewy stink of the fountain. Marilla says it was like getting stabbed in the nose with a rancid hambone.

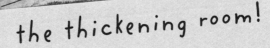

the thickening room!

Freddie shut the door, laughing his head off. The three of us were on the ground. Marilla was curled up into a ball with her coat over her head. Dave says he was fighting to keep from throwing up. I wasn't exactly crying, but tears were coming out. I'm just glad I never actually saw the "grit," whatever that is.

"That's not normally on the tour," said Freddie, between great big hacking laughs, "but I figured you kids deserved a special treat."

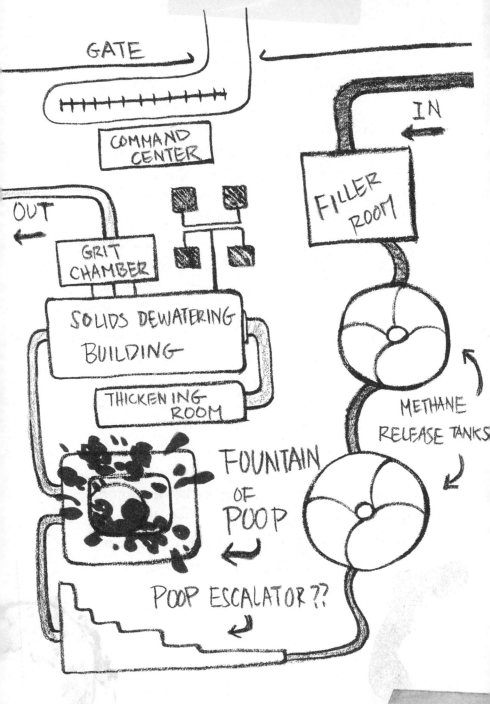

GATE

COMMAND CENTER

IN

OUT

FILLER ROOM

GRIT CHAMBER

SOLIDS DEWATERING BUILDING

THICKENING ROOM

METHANE RELEASE TANKS

FOUNTAIN OF POOP

POOP ESCALATOR??

SECTION XVIII
Farewell to the Fountain

Since Marilla's camera was working again, Freddie took a picture of the three of us next to the fountain. Unfortu nately, I guess Freddie didn't know how to work the camera right, because when we looked at the photos later, it wasn't there! So, after all that, we don't actually have a picture of the poop fountain! Not that we'll ever forget what it looked like. Anyway we held up our pennies for the picture, but Freddie asked us not to throw them into the fountain. One of his employees would end up having to clean them out of a filter sooner or later, he said.

Marilla wanted to make a speech. She said she had been thinking about what to say ever since we first saw the poop fountain in action.

Here is what she said:

Oh, fecal fountain,
time has passed you by.
But we'll remember how
your poop did fly.
Your song will play on
in our hearts evermore,
though your chocolate
waters will dance no more.

-Marilla

I thought Freddie was going to die. We were all laughing, but he was laughing so hard, he started wheezing and hacking and coughing. Finally he sat down on the edge of the fountain and wiped tears from his eyes.

He insisted that Marilla write it down for him. We went back to the command center and she wrote it out in fancy cursive letters just like the copy she made for this report. Then he pinned it in the middle of a bulletin board in the command center and he said he would drive us back to the trailer park.

We all climbed in his truck, which was actually an official town truck, and squeezed together in the front seat. It smelled like cigarettes, and there were balled-up fast-food wrappers everywhere.

When he started the truck, this awful music started playing at about a million decibels.

"Let me guess," Marilla yelled. "Molly Hatchet?"

"Heck, yes!" he whooped.

But, right after he started driving, he turned the music off and hit the brakes. A green SUV was coming through the gate.

"Aw, man!" he said. "We're busted."

The driver of the SUV pulled up next to us and rolled down her window. There was a big white seal on the SUV that said: "Town of Crickenburg, Gateway to the Appalachians."

"Sit tight," said Freddie. "I hope I won't have to squeal on you guys."

Dave says he seriously considered jumping out of the truck and running.

Freddie rolled down his window.

"Hi, Brenda. Merry Christmas!"

"Who you got there, Freddie? Trespassers?"

"Naw, just my sister's kids. Gave 'em a little tour and now I'm running them back to the house."

Brenda squinted at us real hard. Somehow I don't think we looked like what she thought Freddie's sister's kids should look like.

"Why is one of your sister's kids wearing town coveralls?" she asked.

"He got cold," said Freddie.

"Mmm-hmm," said Brenda in that way people have of saying mmm-hmm when they really mean "You're a liar."

But then Brenda gave this funny kind of snort laugh and almost smiled.

"Well, whatever," said Brenda. "I'm just down here to get the wood chipper from the maint enance barn. Got to start grinding up Christmas trees tomorrow."

And she started to drive off.

"Merry Christmas," yelled Freddie, and he drove off too. Fast.

"Well, kids, it's a Christmas miracle!" he said. "I guess the Grinch's heart grew three sizes today."

We all three seemed to let out our breath at the same time.

"Geez, Freddie, I hope you don't get into trouble," said Marilla, the only one of us who could say anything.

"Well, it'll probably come up during my next performance review, but once I get you kids home, she'll never be able to prove anything. Well, unless she looks at the security camera."

"<u>SECURITY CAMERA</u>?!" we all hollered at once.

"Relax," said Freddie, "I'm just yanking your chain. We don't even have one."

We came to the stop sign where Crab Creek Road runs into South Franklin Street.

Crab Creek Road

"Where are we going anyway?" asked Freddie.

"Left. Then turn at the Qwikpick," I said, pointing up the street to the turn for the trailer park. My hand was still shaking.

When he pulled into my driveway, he stomped on the parking brake with a loud crik-crik-crik. He turned in the seat and shook all of our hands. We thanked him about a hundred times.

He told us we could come back anytime, as long as we went straight to the command center first. But I really don't know if we will. I'd be glad to see him again, but I think I'd barf if I got the tiniest whiff of that stink.

We watched him drive away, then turned and looked at each other.

"That," said Marilla, "was awesome!"

"Definitely," said Dave. "I don't know why, because it was cold and gross and we almost got sent to jail--"

"--and I've got thorns in my socks," said Marilla.

"—and I'll never be able to eat chocolate again," said Dave.

"—and I almost lost my camera," said Marilla, "and Lyle almost drowned in poop—"

"—and now I think I've got frostbite," I said.

"—and yet," said Dave, "it was totally worth it."

"Totally," said Marilla.

UNOFFICIAL personal note

I thought for a minute about the sensation of my arm being down in the poop and the droplets hitting my face and the smell. But I also thought about being out in the fields and in the woods and free with Marilla and Dave and about the whole great day, which now I can't imagine not having done and which I wouldn't ever ever want to undo. Plus I got that half a hug from Marilla that I can almost still feel and maybe someday I'll get a whole one.

"Totally," I said.

We started to climb the steps to my trailer.

"You know what I just realized, Lyle?" said Dave. "You weren't just covered in poop, there must have been pee in there too."

"Great."

SECTION XIX
Conclusion

My parents were still working, so we went into my bathroom and scrubbed our hands for a long time.

Then Dave and Marilla came down to the trailer park's laundry room with me while I put my clothes in a washing machine.

Then we went down to the Qwikpick. My parents were way too busy to ask us any questions. We sat around in the break room and rehashed every detail of the day and played Ms. Pac-Man and wrote the haikus about the smell while my clothes got clean.

We were starving and there weren't any leftover biscuits, so believe it or not we actually ate the peanut butter and jelly sandwiches, despite the fact that they had been in the presence of the poop fountain.

Later, we rin sed off the wallet and sent it in the mail to Mr. Dillow. We wrote that we found it, but we didn't mention where we found it. We haven't gotten a response yet, much less a reward.

UNOFFICIAL personal note

That's about all there is to tell. I still feel a little queasy sometimes about sneaking into the poop plant. What if I had really drowned in the poop? What if Brenda had gotten us in BIG trouble? Plus, I don't like keeping a secret from my parents. Every once in a while I almost say something about the fields or Freddie or the wallet that would blow the whole thing.

But I'm glad it turned out to be okay that we went. Now I don't even mind hearing about Dave and Marilla's band trips anymore, because there's no way a band trip is as good as this one was.

And even if we had gotten in trouble, it would have still been worth it, because now we're more than just kids who eat together or hang around together—we're The Qwikpick Adventure Society and nobody else at school can say that.

And Marilla's camera is still working fine, although she says it smells just the very tiniest bit like poop.

On New Year's Day, we went back across the field and walked down to the Taco Bell. It wasn't much of an adventure, but we did laugh our heads off when Marilla bit into her burrito and the refried beans squirted out of the bottom and she said, "Solids, anyone?"

We, the members of THE QWIKPICK
ADVENTURE SOCIETY, promise that
this was a true and faithful
account of our trip to the poop
fountain.

Lyle Hertzog

Marilla Anderson

David H. Raskin

Tom Angleberger is the author of the <u>New York Times</u> bestselling Origami Yoda series. He is also the author of <u>Fake Mustache</u> and <u>Horton Halfpott</u>, both Edgar Award nominees. He has worked as a journalist and lives in the Appalachian Mountains of Virginia with his wife. Visit him online at www.origamiyoda.com.